# little Miss Dotty

by Roger Hargreaves

WORLD INTERNATIONAL

Welcome to Nonsenseland!

You may have heard of it!

It's where the trees are red and the grass is blue!

Where dogs wear hats and birds fly backwards!

And where little Miss Dotty lived, in the middle of Whoopee Wood.

## MORE SPECIAL OFFERS
## FOR MR MEN AND LITTLE MISS READERS

In every Mr Men and Little Miss book like this one, <u>and now</u> in the Mr Men sticker and activity books, you will find a special token. Collect six tokens and we will send you a gift of your choice

Choose either a <u>Mr Men</u> or <u>Little Miss</u> poster, <u>or</u> a Mr Men or Little Miss **double sided** full colour bedroom door hanger.

Return this page <u>**with six tokens per gift required**</u> to:

    Marketing Dept., MM / LM, World International Ltd.,
    PO Box 7, Manchester, M19 2HD

Your name:_____ Age: _____

Address: _____

_____

_____Postcode: _____

Parent / Guardian Name (Please Print)_____

**Please tape a 20p coin to your request to cover part post and package cost**

I enclose <u>six</u> tokens per gift, and 20p please send me:-

| Posters:- | Mr Men Poster | ☐ | Little Miss Poster | ☐ |
|---|---|---|---|---|
| Door Hangers - | Mr Nosey / Muddle | ☐ | Mr Greedy / Lazy | ☐ |
| | Mr Tickle / Grumpy | ☐ | Mr Slow / Busy | ☐ |
| **20p** | Mr Messy / Quiet | ☐ | Mr Perfect / Forgetful | ☐ |
| | L Miss Fun / Late | ☐ | L Miss Helpful / Tidy | ☐ |
| | L Miss Busy / Brainy | ☐ | L Miss Star / Fun | ☐ |

Stick 20p here please

*Please Tick Appropriate Box*

We may occasionally wish to advise you of other Mr Men gifts.
If you would rather we didn't please tick this box ☐

├── 100 mm ──┤

ENTRANCE FEE
3 SAUSAGES

250 mm

**MR.GREEDY**

Collect six of these tokens
You will find one inside every
Mr Men and Little Miss book
which has this special offer.

1
TOKEN

Offer open to residents of UK, Channel Isles and Ireland only

# Mr Men and Little Miss Library Presentation Boxes

In response to the many thousands of requests for the above, we are delighted to advise that these are now available direct from ourselves,
for only £4.99 (inc VAT) plus 50p p&p.
The full colour boxes accommodate each complete library. They have an integral carrying handle as well as a neat stay closed fastener.
Please do not send cash in the post. Cheques should be made payable to **World International Ltd. for the sum of £5.49 (inc p&p)** per box.

**Please note books are not included.**

Please return this page with your cheque, stating below which presentation box you would like, to:-
**Mr Men Office, World International
PO Box 7, Manchester, M19 2HD**

Your name:_____

Address: _____

_____

_____Postcode: _____

Name of Parent/Guardian (please print):_____

Signature:_____

I enclose a cheque for £_____ made payable to World International Ltd.,

Please send me a Mr Men Presentation Box ☐

Little Miss Presentation Box ☐  (please tick or write in quantity)
and allow 28 days for delivery

*Thank you*

**Offer applies to UK, Eire & Channel Isles only**

Nonsenseland really is quite the most extraordinary place.

If you ever come across a worm wearing a straw boater and wearing a bow tie, you'll know you are in Nonsenseland!

And, if you ever happen to catch sight of a pig playing tennis, you'll know exactly where you are!

Won't you?

That's right!

Nonsenseland.

One morning, in January, little Miss Dotty was having breakfast.

A bowlful of marmalade, with milk and sugar!

While she ate, she was reading the newspaper.

She took the Nonsenseland Daily News every day, and always read it while she ate her dotty breakfast.

Something in the paper caught her eye!

She stopped eating and started reading.

The headline read:

'NONSENSE CUP WINNER'

And, underneath, it said:

'This year's Nonsense Cup, for the silliest idea of the year (a green tree), was yesterday awarded to Mr Silly by the King of Nonsenseland. Runners-up were Mr Muddle and Mrs Nincompoop.'

'Next year', continued the story, 'the Nonsense Cup will be awarded, not for the silliest idea, but for the DOTTIEST idea of the year.'

"The dottiest idea of the year?" little Miss Dotty thought to herself as she popped a spoonful of marmalade into her mouth. "I bet I could win that Nonsense Cup!"

After breakfast she set off for a walk in Whoopee Wood to think about this and that, but most of all to think about that famous Nonsense Cup.

On her walk she met Mr Silly.

"Congratulations on winning the Cup," she said to him.

"Oh, it was nothing really," he replied, modestly.

Little Miss Dotty thought about telling him that she was going to enter next year, but then she decided not to.

January passed.

And February.

And spring came, and the blue grass grew.

But, could little Miss Dotty think of an idea?

She could not!

She just couldn't think of a single
dotty idea!

Summer came to Nonsenseland.

And went!

Without a single dotty idea in mind!

And the red leaves started to fall from the trees.

And then, one afternoon in late November, little Miss Dotty thought of her idea.

The dottiest idea ever!

The year ended, and January arrived in Nonsenseland.

A huge crowd gathered as usual in the Square to see who had won that year's Nonsense Cup.

The King of Nonsenseland mounted the specially built platform, and a hush descended on the crowd.

"Ladies and gentlemen," the King announced. "Again it is my pleasure to announce the annual winner of our famous Nonsense Cup."

"As you know," he continued, "the Cup will be awarded this year to whoever has had the dottiest idea of the year!"

The crowd held its breath.

"One of which," the King went on, "has been entered by Mr Nonsense!"

The crowd looked as Mr Nonsense held up his dotty idea for all to see.

A television set, with no screen!

"It's for people who don't like watching television," he explained, proudly.

The crowd clapped.

"However," continued the King, "we have an even dottier idea from last year's winner!"

Mr Silly triumphantly showed his invention to the crowd.

It was a clock!

"If you look at it in the mirror it tells you the right time," he announced.

The crowd cheered, and Mr Silly felt sure that he was going to win the Nonsense Cup for the second year running.

"But," continued the King, and Mr Silly realised that he wasn't.

"But," said the King again. "We did announce that the Nonsense Cup was to be awarded for the DOTTIEST idea of the year, and this year's winner has provided us with," he paused, "nine hundred and ninety nine DOTS!!"

Little Miss Dotty held her breath, and blushed.

"Hurrah!" roared the crowd.

"Follow me," said the King.

The King and little Miss Dotty led the crowd through Whoopee Wood to her cottage.

And there they stopped, and stared.

Little Miss Dotty had spent the whole month of December painting dots all over her cottage. Hundreds and hundreds of different coloured dots.

Nine hundred and ninety nine to be exact.

Little Miss Dotty had counted them, very carefully.

"That's a lot of dots," remarked the King as he handed over the Nonsense Cup, and the crowd cheered.

"Thank you your Majesty," she replied, and she blushed with pride.

Oh, one last thing!

If you are as good at counting dots as little Miss Dotty, you'll be interested to know that there are one hundred and eighty three small letter 'i's' in this story.

And, there are one hundred and eighty three dots on the top of all of them!

I should know!

Because I put them there!